D0244102

804 000 0029433

FOR MY GODSON,
(KING) ARTHUR

x

Waltham Forest Libraries

904 000 00294534

Askews & Holts	07-Mar-2014
PIC	£6.99
4224468	S

First published in 2014 by Scholastic Children's Books
Euston House, 24 Eversholt Street
London NW1 1DB
a division of Scholastic Ltd
www.scholastic.co.uk
London ~ New York ~ Toronto ~ Sydney ~ Auckland
Mexico City ~ New Delhi ~ Hong Kong

Text and Illustrations copyright © 2014 Alex T. Smith

HB ISBN 978 1407 13847 3
PB ISBN 978 1407 13848 0

All rights reserved
Printed in Singapore

1 3 5 7 9 10 8 6 4 2

The moral rights of Alex T. Smith have been asserted.

Papers used by Scholastic Children's Books are made from wood grown in sustainable forests.

SCHOLASTIC

*T*he tiny village

of Spottybottom

was a **lovely** place to live.

Everyone knew everyone, and
nothing bothersome **ever** happened.

That was until the day Hector's Granny had her **magic wand** stolen by the

Big

Bad

Knight...

And the Big Bad Knight laughed,

"Ha~ha! You'll never catch me!
I'm the biggest, baddest knight
you ever did see."

And he galloped away
with Granny's magic wand.

"Don't worry, Granny," said Hector.
"I'll get your wand back for you!"

All the villagers laughed!

"You?" they giggled,

"But you're tiny and small!
And your spindly arms have no muscles at all!"

But Hector had a plan...

He packed a hanky with Useful Things and set off with his friend Norman to rescue the magic wand.

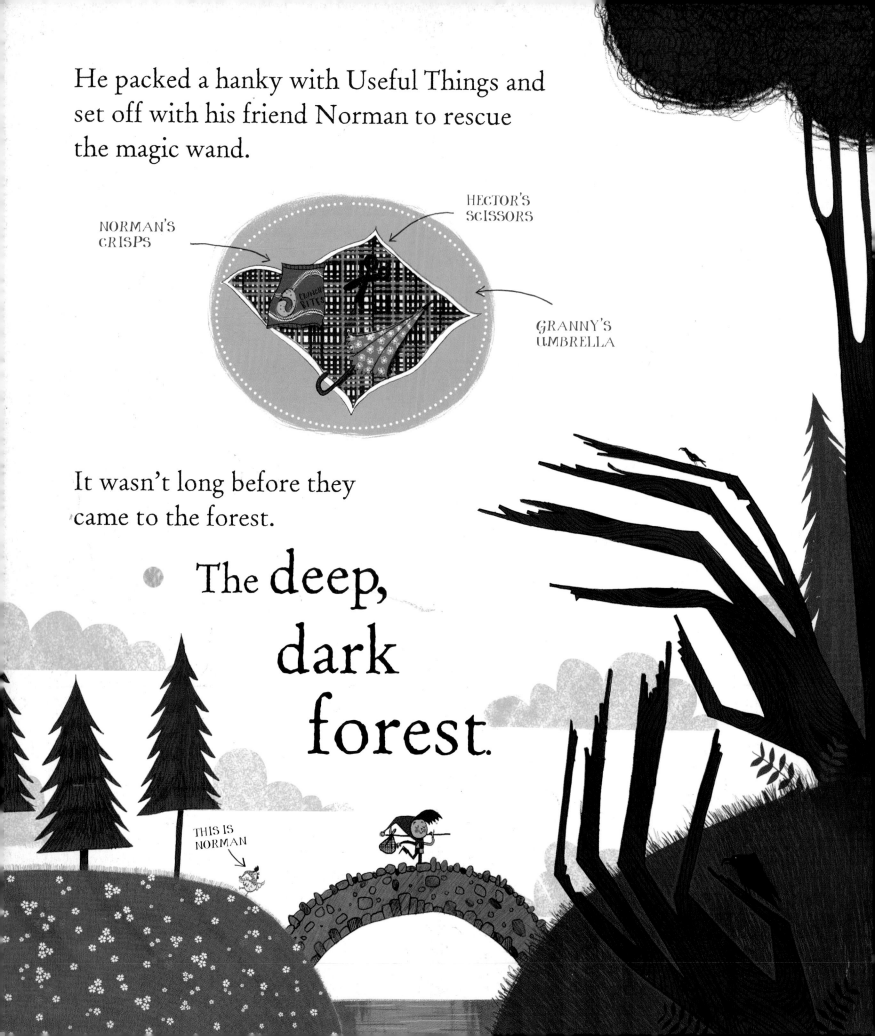

NORMAN'S CRISPS

HECTOR'S SCISSORS

GRANNY'S UMBRELLA

It wasn't long before they came to the forest.

The deep, dark forest.

THIS IS NORMAN

And in the deep, dark forest
the Big Bad Knight stopped
and twirled Granny's wand.
With a sprinkle of magic, giant,
thorny weeds sprang up.

"You'll never climb that –
it's tangly and tall!
And as we all know,
you're tiny and small!"

But Hector
had a plan...

With a snip, snip, snip of his scissors...

SNIP! SNIP! SNIP!

...Hector and Norman were free.

"Uh-oh," squeaked the Big Bad Knight...

...and he trotted off to the **moat**.

ABSOLUTELY NO SWIMMING!

The dark, dingy moat.

And at the dark, dingy moat the Big Bad Knight stopped and twirled Granny's wand.

With a sprinkle of magic, the **drawbridge disappeared.**

oh!

The Big Bad Knight
chuckled...

"You'll **never** cross this moat –
not even with a **leap**.
You'll end up in the water,
dangerous
and
deep!"

But
Hector
had a plan.

"Uh-oh," groaned the Big Bad Knight, and he clip-clopped away up the castle tower.

The terribly **tall** tower.

Hector and Norman quickly followed.

Up on the roof of the terribly tall tower
the Big Bad Knight hollered...

"Well, you've got this far,
But you'll never trick me.
I'm a super clever knight,
just you wait and see!"

And he stopped and twirled Granny's wand.
With a sprinkle of magic,
he turned his
horse into...

...a dragon.

A humongous, hungry hungry dragon!

And the Big Bad Knight giggled,

"This peckish beast will eat you in a flash.
You should run away! Quick! Make a dash!"

But the Dragon had a plan.

"Eat **Hector** up?
He'd hardly be a bite.
So I think instead I'll gobble up
the **Big Bad Knight!**"

Ooh! LOVELY!

Hector leapt into **action**.

He threw Norman's **crisps** to the dragon and then grabbed the **magic wand** back with a

SWIPE!

Back in Spottybottom, Hector's Granny hooted,

"Three cheers for Hector who's so tiny and so small!
He got my wand back for me — he's the bravest of them all!"

But Granny wasn't sure what to do with the Big Bad Knight.
He had been **very naughty** and needed to learn a lesson.

Luckily Hector
had a plan...

...a very STINKY plan!

DRAGON POOP FOR SALE! GOOD FOR YOUR GARDEN.

Dragon Poop

The End

Already?